Chronicles of The Black Rose of Kush

The Seven Golden Queens

Ras Lazarus Nazari

Cover designed by Christina D. Jones

Art by Benjamin Green

TheBlackRoseOfKushFilms@gmail.com

Copyright © 2017 by Ras Lazarus Nazari

ISBN: 9781549529016

CONTENTS

CHAPTER ONE: THE ULTIMA RATIO REGUM

It was the first of the month and Den Night Club was rockin' like a boat on the sea, packed from wall to wall. It was the same old local crowd with a few new college girls taking advantage of the cool, breezy summer night in Savannah, Georgia. The players were buying drinks and the first of the month checks had everyone looking like stars. By this time of night, the different sets usually got so rowdy that fights broke out, but tonight was different.

Before the tear-the-club-up hour came, a six-foot Beyoncé look-alike, with a little African look, walked in the club and everyone froze. She was the perfect quarter piece. Her hips could rock a baby to sleep. Her breasts would make a baby cry from just seeing them. And her eyes had a hazel fire that stopped men like deer in headlights. As she made her way to the bar, the crowd parted for her like the Red Sea, except for the few guys trying to get a little bump and eye contact. It was obvious that everyone was thinking the same thing--she had to be in the wrong place.

"Can I have a Nuvo and Alizé mixed?" she asked.

"Only if you tell me your name and show me you over 21," answered Jesse James, the bartender and owner of Den.

"Now if you didn't have the wedding ring on, I would show you I'm over 21, but my name is Vanity, and I hope my smile is grown enough 'cause I don't have I.D."

"Well that idea is grown enough 'cause I almost took my ring off, but my wife at the other end of the bar, so I'm just going to fix your drink before I change my status," he said, looking like a hypnotized victim.

"Why they sweating that bitch? She probably the damn police," Shante said, easing her way over to the bar next to Vanity to see who was going to try and buy the new girl the first drink.

"Oh my God! Your nails are so tight! Who did them?" Vanity asked, looking down at Shante's hands.

"Girl, this nothing. I do it myself," Shante answered, smiling.

"Do you have a shop? 'Cause I'd pay to get mine done like that. Oh, excuse me, my name is Vanity. Sorry I didn't introduce myself before I got all in your nails."

"No problem, I was being nosey too. Seeing which sucker gonna come frontin' on you first like he got money." They dapped and laughed.

"Shoot, girl you sound like my sister. She real just like you, but I'm here to get money. Ain't no fakin' me. I'm gonna find the strip club and try and get it all," said Vanity.

"Girl you dance? You too pretty for that. 'Specially in this town's hole in the wall clubs." Shante tapped her girl Tina.

"Yeah, ain't nothing in the hole in the wall but bullet holes, stretch marks, and ex-junkies," said Tina, Shante's right-hand girl and shoplifting partner.

"Damn, that means I'll get all the money. If you show me around and turn me on to ballers, I'll look out. Plus, I do need someone to smoke this OG Kush with, too," Vanity said with a hood smirk and hip wind.

"Girl, you talking my language!" said ole' thirsty throat Shante as Eddy Love walked up. "What's up, ladies? May I buy you a drink?" he asked.

"Of course you may," said Tina with an old English accent.

"Tina, I know you want me to, but I'm talking to...I didn't get your name," Eddy said to Vanity.

"Ed, now that was really a tired ass way to ask her name. All that proper shit. Just say what you want fool. Your scary ass."

"What you mean, Shante? I'm just seeing if I can buy her—"

"—Go buy your baby mama and kids something! You faking! Plus, she cost too much for your broke ass!"

Shante grabbed Vanity's hand and led her to a table. Vanity made full hood approval, for she made the number one hater her partner and that was pure hood respect. Shante only respected the true bosses and the real money getters, so now everyone was watching. Vanity ordered her and her new girls a bottle of Moet to celebrate their new friendship and they took it to the bathroom.

"Girl, when your Beyoncé looking ass came in the club, I said 'look at that ole' stuck up bitch.' I never thought you'd be in the bathroom smoking a blunt like a real hood chick. Shit...girl, you will fool a muthafucka," Shante said and they all laughed.

"This is the real Kush, Shante," said Tina.

"Where you get it from, girl?" asked Shante.

"This is California's finest. I got an old rich dude who looks out for me," Vanity said, inhaling.

"I am *so* high. So where you staying at, Vanity?" Shante asked.

"Sounds like you two ready to go now. Well, I have a room at the Best Western, but my old Italian trick will be in town soon. So I'll be staying in his house. Y'all wanna go to the room with me and finish this blunt?" Vanity asked.

"Girl, you too damn down. You ain't the police, are you?" asked Tina.

"Yeah, I am the police, smoking with you in a bathroom," said Vanity, laughing.

"You really gay and just wanna eat some pussy. Is that it? I never been with a woman before, but you a pretty muthafucka and I'd be lying if I said I wasn't wondering how pretty your body must be," said Tina.

"This must be some good shit 'cause Tina you talking like you trying to come out, and I ain't with that shit. But if you two want to, then don't look for me. I'll just smoke and watch," said Shante, passing the blunt back to Vanity.

"Listen, Tina. I do go both ways, but I am not hitting on you. If we get tingly, then maybe. But I just wanna kick it, trip, and smoke. You don't owe me nothing. But I do like the way your breasts look, so I'd be lying if I didn't say that I thought about sucking them," Vanity said before reaching over to touch Tina's chest. Tina and Shante laughed as they all got up to leave.

"Aw man, the girl gay. I knew it was too good to be true," Eddy said after witnessing Vanity touch Tina's breasts.

"Ed, what you mean it's too good to be true?" asked C.W.

"Yeah, Ed. You say that like you been in," added Fresh.

"Man, when I went and hollered at her, she was supposed to get with me, but hating Tina was blocking. I still got her number though," Eddy said, finishing his drink.

"You lying like a fuck, Ed," said Skeeta.

"Skeeta, you hatin' too," said Ed.

"Well, Ed...what the girl name is?" Skeeta asked, folding his arms.

"What, so you can backdoor me? Find out yourself."

"You don't know, your fronting ass," said Skeeta.

"Man, the girl name is...is...is Rachel like the B.E.T old Island music video chick. She from the Islands too," said Ed.

"I told you! I told you this a frontin' ass nigga. Why you front so much? You know when you lie on your dick, it gets smaller. Ed, you ain't fucking nothing with your tired ass proper English game. The bitch is *Vanity*. Yes, Vanity like the damn old ass singer who had Prince fucked up," said Skeeta.

"So you expect me to believe that she told you, Skeeta, her name?" Eddy asked, trying to defend his last bit of pride.

"Nah, bitch ass nigga. If I talked to her, I would have told her I got $200 for her fine ass and that was that. Then you would have seen me fucking. But her name is on the front of her BMW out in the parking lot, Jackass." Everyone laughed at Ed, shaking their heads.

"Skeeta, let's go. Pam got her girl April and they ready to do this," said C.W before grabbing his drink and downing, while still shaking his head at Ed.

CHAPTER TWO: VANITY'S VANITY

The next morning, the girls woke up in the same bed, naked and laughing. The hotel maid woke them up when she came in the door, but ran out when she saw that it was three women in the bed.

"What was that?" asked Shante.

"What do you mean? That was the maid," said Tina.

"No, I mean what happened last night. I felt like I got possessed. It even felt like a man was here with us. It was magical, but I can't...I can't call it," said Shante.

"It's just good energy and sexual pleasure to a higher degree. And Shante you kiss so passionately," said Vanity as she caressed Tina's breast. They rolled over from next to each other.

"I can't lie...I came like a running hose and my shit is still jumping now. Fuck, I may be gay 'cause my shit don't jump like that with dick. Vanity, not to be disrespectful, but you a pussy eating muthafucka and I say that with the highest respect." Shante said and they all laughed.

Vanity crawled over and kissed Shante on her belly button.

"Bitch, I'ma have to get away from you 'cause you tryin' to possess me. It feels like you working roots," said Shante as she jumped up out of bed to go to the bathroom. Tina popped her on the ass.

"Girl, I told you to stop being scary. It's just sex. Don't get scared if you like it. You liked it?"

"Well, we were high and that played a role. But don't get me wrong, I love men and a woman is only foreplay to me. So Shante, we just friends and I am not trying to turn you out, okay?" Vanity yelled across the room.

"I hear you, Vanity, but I knew your ass had a plan when we left that club, but played right into it. And no, I ain't mad that I tried it, Tina. It's just that this shit could be addictive and an ole nasty bitch like me don't need no more addictions 'cause dick bad enough," Shante said, stepping in the shower.

Tina and Vanity laughed. Then Tina led Vanity to the bathroom to shower with Shante to rinse away their morning's session.

"I let you two freaky hoes get me again," Shante said as she dried off.

"Vanity, we ain't gon' be doing this all day. I'm like Shante now, my shit jumping too much. I can't take it," Tina said.

"Nah, girls I thought we would go shopping now and get us something to eat. I got one of my trick's credit cards and I plan to max...it...*out*, so are y'all down? 'Cause I don't mind buying my girls something too. Plus, we should get our hair and nails done like ballers," said Vanity.

"Bitch, I started to tell you I love you, but you'd probably be in here eating pussy again, so I'm down," Shante said as they dapped and laughed.

"Well fire her up, Tina," Vanity said, wiggling into her jeans.

"After we finish shopping, we can stop to Miss Sula and get something to eat there. It's Sunday, so the ballers will definitely be in the building," said Shante.

The girls hit the town wide open—first in the mall, then downtown. They got their hair and nails done, plus massages. By 7:30 that evening, they headed down to the Southside of Savannah to an area called Pinpoint. There was a lady named Mama Sula who cooked dinners that are famous all up the east coast. Everything from fried fish to gumbo to turkey wings. Fried chicken, the famous Savannah devil crabs, and everything else.

Needless to say, Miss Sula's was the place to be.

"Now, Vanity you say you the truth," Shante challenged.

"Well, we going where the real of real is at. If you looking for money, these the ones," she added, shaking her head.

"Girl, just get me in there and you watch the madam at work," Vanity boasted as she whips her BMW up in the front to valet parking, so her and her new girls could hop out looking Hollywood.

"Oh, it's still a good bit of people here too," Shante said as they pulled up in the driveway.

"Shit, that's C.W....and *Splack*. He got it too, but he usually only deal with out of town girls. So Vanity he might go right at you, 'cause he don't give us locals the time of day."

"Oh shit! Ain't that Big Al car, the Benz in the cut?" Tina asked.

"Yeah, girl. Now Vanity the test is here, but they all here at once. You got to handle that," Shante said, fixing her hair in the mirror.

"Baby, men are like babies. Each just need a little feeding time and I can rock them to sleep. They don't care about the other man as long as they get their feeding time," Vanity said, winking at Tina in the mirror. She had the confidence of a predator.

As they get out the car, the scent of soul food filled the air and hints of Kush seeped from a parked car with low bass beating from its trunk.

"Yeah, I feel him near," Vanity said, smirking.

"What you mean you feel him?" Tina asked, mesmerized by Vanity.

"No, I mean the music in the car, girl," Vanity said, stepping aside so the girls could lead her inside.

"Hey, girls how y'all doing today?" Mama Sula greeted them.

"Alright," Tina and Shante answered, giving Mama Sula a hug.

"Oh, who this pretty something y'all got with y'all. Them boys must be ain't seen her yet 'cause they would be all over her." Mama Sula had no shame.

"Hello, Mama Sula. My name is Vanity and I can't wait to try your deviled crab. I've heard all about them," Vanity said.

"Aww shit, Miss Proper. Girl, let me fix your plate now 'cause in a minute, they ain't gon' let you breathe. So what else you want?"

"Ummm...macaroni, candy yams, a little rice, Devil crab, and is that banana pudding?" Vanity asked.

"Yes, baby. I got you," Mama Sula said.

"Oh, Tina...You and Shante want the regular?"

"Yes ma'am," they answered.

Splack walked in the kitchen and looked Vanity up and down. "Girl, you look like trouble," he said before walking out the door.

"I am...for a *weak mind*," Vanity said, defending herself.

Splack looked back in the door. "Come out here and let me talk to you, trouble for a weak mind."

Vanity followed him outside. "What's up?" she asked.

"What you want it to be? Team drafting or just playing a one-day draft?" Splack had the swagger of a pimp.

"$800. No cuts, no shorts, and I'm a day draft. All-star player for you 'til you tell me you can't take it no more."

Vanity had the eyes of a seductress and knew exactly how to work them. "You so damn pretty, you scare me a little. So I'm going to follow my gut. What do you really want? 'Cause you driving a six-series BMW, you got shopping bags in the car, your hair done, and you been using plastic all day in the malls, as the word is. So you looking for something other than trick money for an $800 spot 'cause that ain't gon' carry you. So what do you want for real?"

"You a real thinker, so I'll give it to you raw. I want blood," she answered with a smile.

"Tell me for real and this may work in your advantage."

"Okay, I have a few chips, but I love sex and the danger of the game. I guess you can say I am a nympho. Plus, let's say I am looking for the winning team to get down with." She touched his chest then grabbed his hand. She slowly placed his hand on her breast and added, "I'd love to make you holler."

Splack licked his lips. "9:30. Hit me. Put this number in your phone: 305-772-6775. And be by yourself too."

"That's a Miami number," she said confused.

"Yeah, I have many residences. Is that a problem?" asked Splack.

"Nah, just making sure it wasn't fake," Vanity said. Not giving him a chance to respond, she walked back to the house.

"Girl, I see you", Tina said.

"I told you," Mama Sula said, handing Vanity her plate. Vanity give her a $20 bill and told her to keep the change.

"Oh shit, Shante! I like this girl! But, baby, your eyes trouble me a little. Come here, let me ask you something," Mama Sula said to Vanity.

Vanity walked over and sat in front of Mama Sula.

"Child, you carrying something heavy and you that kind of beautiful most people ain't going to see. Pain makes us all do funny things, but it's never too late to come back over. You may say *this old lady talkin' crazy*, but this old spirit sees past the flesh and listens to souls. So when the time come, you remember what I tell you. Nothing can wash the pain away unless you stop living through it. Girl, we were once great Queen Mothers. True givers of life, but you will have to find that again. Now these words are called a reading for you. I can't feed your body, but not your mind and soul. So now you can say 'old Mama Sula fed me.'"

She got up to fix the next plate.

"Girl, Mama Sula don't do no reading until she feels you. So you something special," Shante said, taking a seat next to Vanity.

"Alright, Vanity I asked Big Al if you could dance in his club. He was trippin' when I said you dance. So go holla at him," Tina said, pushing her to get up and go to the back of the house.

Vanity followed Tina to the back where there was a 72" flat screen surrounded by men watching the game. The noise quieted to just a stare when they saw Vanity. Then Tina pointed to Big Al.

"What's up, Big Al?" Vanity said, sitting on the arm of his chair.

Big Al froze up. "Well, umm I hear you dance," he said.

"Well, do you want me to?" she asked, clearly aware that he was blown away by her.

"You talking like you ready now," he said, rubbing his pants legs.

"That's because I am, Big Al." She stood up and untied her dress around her neck, letting it drop to the floor in front of Big Al.

"Shit, now she done fucked me up," said Willie B as he eased in for a closer look.

"Don't touch unless you can pay," Tina said, stepping in like she was Vanity's bodyguard.She leaned in close to his ear. Her nipple brushed the side of his arm.

"Do I have a job or do you need me to perform?"

"Nah, you perfect. Damn, you perfect," he said.

Satisfied, Vanity readjusted her dress. "I'll see you Tuesday," she said, walking off with Tina.

"*You perfect*," Willie B. mocked.

"What the fuck was that, Al? The girl was ready to put in work and your ass talkin' about she perfect."

"She is bad as hell. Shit, I was fucked up too," said C.W.

"Shit, I ain't gon' lie. I just realized what the bitch was sayin' about performing. Shit, them headlights was in my face and her eyes just gaze out like... Shit, the bitch damn near so beautiful, she looks evil," said Big Al.

"One thing I know, I will be to Big Al's Tuesday night on the front row with a pocketful," said Skeeta.

"Alright, Mama Sula...I'll see you next week and I heard you, too," Vanity said, paying her respects as she and Shante walked out to the car.

"Okay, baby. Y'all be careful. You know these niggas out here crazy and being beautiful like you are don't always help," Mama Sula said, waving.

"Where Tina?" asked Vanity as they got in the car.

"Oh, she gone with her baby daddy. That was the boy Splack's little cousin Nardy. The one with the pretty dark skin and the Mohawk."

"Oh yeah, he cut his eyes at me too," said Vanity.

"Girl, he a trip, but don't sweat him," Shante said.

"So you hanging with me tonight or what?" Vanity asked, smiling.

"Nah, girl. My sister gon' charge me about four hair do's and probably her nails too for keeping my kids all this time," said Shante.

"You have kids? As in more than one?" Vanity asked.

"Yeah, girl. I am not only a mother, but a grandmother. I have an 18-year-old son and two daughters. My daughter Yalonda is 10 and my daughter Sunday is 5, and they don't listen to no one but their brother, Jahmel," Shante said, showing her arm tattoos.

"But you can come to my house and chill. If you got something to smoke, we can smoke. Shit, I got to introduce you to my sister anyway. She bartends at Big Al's."

"Okay, I'm down. Shit, you know I am game 'cause I see Big Al slow as a muthafucka, so I may be running the spot soon," Vanity said pulling out of the spot.

"Girl, you crazy. Big Al just a minor player in that club. Some major players finance the spot with him, so don't play yourself. These some dangerous guys now," warned Shante.

"Shante, I am the most gangster bitch you will ever meet. Anyways, I just want their blood," said Vanity.

"Bitch, what you mean blood? What you got that ninja?"

"The Ninja? What is that?"

"Bitch, don't play with me. I will fuck you up. You know what the hell the Ninja is," Shante said as she raises up in her seat placing her back on the door for fight mood.

"Please, Shante...I really don't," Vanity said, laughing.

"The Ninja, riding with no helmet, like what we did the other night. The package. The AIDS, BITCH!", says Shante as she went from looking pissed to looking scared.

"No, Shante. I don't have no disease. It's just a term I use to describe my taste for life in life," Vanity said, still laughing.

"That shit ain't funny. You sound like you came to kill something," said Shante, looking confused.

Vanity reached over between Shante's legs and rubbed her clit. "I'm so glad you didn't wear panties 'cause the only thing I want to kill is that dryness. I want it to jump every time you see me," she moaned.

"I want to kill the loneliness that I know you feel," Vanity said, seductively.

"Bitch, I told you ain't no turning me out. I love dick and *lick lick lick* is good, but I ain't eating no pussy. So let me say this: Beware, my baby daddy is crazy and jealous of girls too and will act up if he hears this, so don't give no signs at my house. Please," Shante said, damn near begging. She closed her legs as Vanity turned in her Carver Village driveway.

"Okay, Shante. I understand," said Vanity, smirking.

CHAPTER THREE: THE MOVES

After several hours of chilling with Shante and her family, Vanity thought about Splack.

"Damn, I almost forgot I have the young, cutie Splack's number. We supposed to get up. What you think about him, Shante?"

"He a hard one to figure out at times, but he real smooth though. A real Southside Geechee. They believe in roots and things like that. Some girls say them Geechees put works on 'em. I don't know, but he gets money," Shante said, finishing the last braid of her daughter's hair.

The money was all she needed to hear. Vanity excused herself. "Shit, he didn't answer." Almost immediately, her phone rung.

"Oh, you called back," she said.

He got straight to the point. "Hyatt Hotel, room 212 and like I said, no one else." He hung up.

"This dude just gave orders and hung up. He a trip, but I like his swag. I got to go to the Hyatt, Shante, but I'll call you in the morning."

"Okay girl, but call me when you touch down and when you leave to let me know you good," Shante said sounding like a real Mom.

"I got you. Oh yeah, I left a nice bud on your dresser too," Vanity said before closing the front door behind her.

As Vanity rides off, her phone rings. Then a voice of an old Italian-like accent on the other end of the line said, "Hello, my dear. I hope everything is going well. I sense that you've grown close to them already. I know you like to play, but don't get lost in your fun. The time is growing close."

"Yes, I understand and I will provide," Vanity answered.

"Good, I'll see you soon," he said then hung up.

Vanity turned up the volume on Kid Cudi's "Day and Night." Speeding and vibing down the highway, she began to cry. She took the blunt out the ashtray and fired it up. The GPS alerted her to make the next exit. In less than five minutes, she pulled into the parking lot of the hotel. Instead of rushing inside, she parked the car and smoked her blunt until it was small enough to burn the tips of her fingers. Now leveled, she pulled her cellphone out of her purse and called Splack.

"Downstairs. I'll be up in a few."

As she made her way upstairs and down the hall, she smelled a funny scent. The closer she got to the door, the stronger the smell got. She knocked anyway. Splack opened the door and stepped aside.

"Come on in," he said.

"What's that smell?" she asked.

"Three Kings incense," he said, picking up the blunt out the ashtray. "Why? Does it bother you?" He asked, studying her.

"A little, but I'm cool," she said, kneeling down in front of Splack. On cue, he leaned back in his chair and licked his lips. She rubbed his thigh and gently moved her hand to his zipper. With her thumb, she massaged his foreskin, using his precum as natural lubrication. With her other hand, she began pleasing herself. Her eyes locked on his, she removed her fingers from her clit and sucked on each one individually. It was so good, she moaned.

Splack stood up and unbuckled his pants. Vanity followed suit, relocating his hands to her ass. She began kissing his neck and slowly worked her way down, easing his pants off in one clean motion. As she planted kisses around his thighs, Splack began to moan. She paused to reach for a condom. Like pro, she put it in her mouth, worked it down his shaft, and began sucking his dick. Her hand and mouth had a rhythm of their own, moving like ocean waves, as she caressed his balls with her other hand. Sensing the rise in him, she increased the tempo, and just as he was about to reach the point of climax, she stopped.

"Remember when I said that I wanted to make you holler?" she asked, pushing him back onto the bed.

"I'm ready now. Have you ever had sex that was a little...too good? I mean so good that you had to beg her to stop?"

He shook his head no. She smiled. That was exactly what she wanted to hear. As cool natured as he was, he couldn't contain his excitement. That turned her on even more. Mind, body and spirit were aligned with one goal: fucking. Hardcore fucking. He couldn't recall the last time his dick had been that hard. The last time he'd wanted someone so bad.

"I want to make you beg me to stop. Lay back and now close your eyes," she said, stepping out of her dress. She picked up where she'd left off at and Splack wasted no time reaching his climax. Naturally, his dick began to go down.

"Oh no, I know you got more for me," Vanity said, taking the rubber off.

She then put another in her mouth and resumed sucking his dick. Splack moaned for her to hold up. Instead, she got more aggressive. Once he was fully aroused again, she climbed on top of him and began to grind slowly. He felt himself rising again as her hips rocked back and forth. She threw her head back and moaned as she squeezed her inner muscles up the length of his dick. She planted her feet firmly on the bed and began grinding harder. Slowly, she rose to the tip of his dick, stopped, and then gripped the head with her well-trained muscles. Splack almost didn't recognize his own voice as he moaned louder.

"Girl, you trying to fuck me up?" He asked, feeling himself about to cum again. As if she didn't hear him, she kept going. Kept grinding and popping and squeezing and thrusting and moaning. It was too much. She lifted her head and made eye contact with him. Biting her bottom lip, she began rubbing her clit. Growing more excited, she rode faster. He tried to slow her down, but she was out of control. He began jerking and she got up, took the rubber off, and jacked his dick. He released all over her breasts.

"Shit, girl...You almost gave me a mean ass cramp, I was bracing so much."

"You know, I thought your fuck game would have been a little better, but it was nice," she said, getting up.

"Well I can say, Miss Vanity, you do have a biter. It ain't all tore up, so you do take care of yourself. But your touch is like fucking...*magic*," he said, following her to the bathroom.

"Oh no, Mr. Splack! Don't do the lover thing. This just business. So please, no cuddling 'cause it will make you soft," she said, removing his hands from around her waist.

"I feel you. Your money on the table, Baby girl. So if this was to be a team draft, what would that take?" he asked.

"Really, I like killers. Coldhearted thugs with no love who'll do whatever. That shit makes my pussy jump and bow to them," she said in an evil yet seductive tone.

"Well, I'm a mama's boy. I just don't do that cold shit. I do the spiritual thing, but I see you cold for real. My mama says a person who can't take the smell of Three Kings got a dark spirit on them. I sense that when you first came in, but your beauty blinded me to just how cold you really are. So don't worry, baby. You not my type of team either. If I need a nut, I'll call."

"Shit! Splack, you made me get wet with that gangster tone then. You lost the softness. I knew you had it in you. Now let's talk beyond fucking and petty money. I want a real team to do a job with me. Like you said, tricking ain't gonna pay my bills," she said with the look of a mobster.

"What you mean 'a job'?" he asked cautiously.

"I got an old Italian boss who calls me to his house, and when I say he got it...*he got it*. But I need a team for this lick," she said.

"When you say 'got it,' what you talkin'? You may not recognize, but chips ain't no problem here. So what do you call a lick?" Splack asked in true street mode.

"I consider chips to be a drop off point for the bosses. At least five million cash and 100 keys of heroin. The mother-load and the lap of the beast," she answered, confidently.

"Sound good, but why would a major boss let you, a prostitute, see or know his business like that?"

"What can I say? This pussy biting and money make it a dick monster. So am I thinking out loud to the right one or have I just wasted my breath with you on this?" she asked.

"If I did decide to get involved, what is your idea of the cut on this?" he asked.

"I just want what every woman wants in a relationship: a 50/50 deal, signed and sealed in blood," she said with her usual seductive smirk.

"Let me think about this and maybe we'll make a round to see the set and I'll tell you then. Take your shower. I might have an answer before you get out."

Vanity gets in the shower and Splack goes and sits down on the bed and pulls his phone out. "MannyBo, where you at?" he whispered into the phone.

"Traveling in the East, What's up?"

"Look, I'm at the Hy, got me. And I got a friend with me. She got a Midnight Black6 series with Vanity on the front. I need you to check her route and we'll talk later."

"One, I got you Homie," MannyBo.

They hung and he sat the phone down beside him. Stretched out on the bed and considered the weight of the convo he'd just had with Vanity. So deep in his thoughts, he didn't see or hear her come out of the bathroom.

"So Mr. Splack...and anyway what is your name for real, if I can ask?"

"This just business right? No lover thing. So names ain't important," he said.

"Yeah, you right," she agreed.

"Look, I'll meet you Tuesday at the club, tell you what can be done, and maybe I'll introduce you to a team of *real thugs* as you say," Splack said. Vanity finished drying off and rubbed herself down in Victoria Secret's

Peaches and Cream lotion. Afterwards, she put her dress back on.

"Well can you hand me a little fun money? And I guess I'll be on my way," she said, grabbing her purse to leave.

Splack handed her $1000. "I shot you an extra $200 for being such an interesting person."

Vanity smiled and kissed him on the cheek before letting herself out. She hummed the entire way back to the parking lot. As instructed, parked three cars down, MannyBo watched her get in the car and pull out. Not long after, he pulled out, and careful not to get caught, he followed her to the Southside in the area of Old Montgomery. Vanity drove into a yard gated in five-foot brick walls with vines snaking throughout the gaps. The house could easily be considered a mini-mansion. As she stepped out to go inside, MannyBo called Splack.

"Well, Family, your hot mama must got some money 'cause she chilling on the Southside Waterfront Mansion. It has a security gate and this just look like old money. Now we been here for years and I never seen her in this area. Why is this information so important?" asked MannyBo.

"It may be your key to retirement. Take a picture with yo cell, if you can, and meet me at the spot," answered Splack.

"One," said MannyBo, hanging up.

Splack called up Bones, another one of his soldiers and told him to meet him at the spot. That night, they all talked about what Vanity said about the money and the Black Tar. They agreed to make the lick and then kill Vanity just in case the mob caught her and pressed her to tell who was behind the lick.

"No mistakes and no one knows but us," warned Splack as they all got ready to leave.

Meanwhile, Vanity made herself comfortable in her hideaway. Waking up from a cat nap, she remembered that she was supposed to call Shante.

"Shante, I forgot to call, but I'm in now."

Shante fussed as if they'd been friends since forever.

"Well I'm calling now. I'm about to get in the tub. I'll come check on you in the morning. Did Tina call you?" Vanity said, changing the subject.

"Yeah, she over here now. Her freaky tail looking for you," Shante said.

Vanity could hear Tina in the background yelling "*She lying!*"

"Tell her I'm blowing her a kiss right now," Vanity said.

"Alright. Well, girl I know you probably tired. So I'll talk to you tomorrow," Shante said.

"Alright. Oh, and I really had a good time with you two," Vanity said before hanging up.

She then lit several candles, the start of her ritual before taking a bath. As the lights flickered from the flames in the dark house, shallow echoes, like voices of souls, bounced in and out. Neck-deep in bubbles and hot water, she fell asleep. As the lights shun against her flawless skin, a dark shadow rose up over her as if staring into her soul.

"I thought I was alone," she said waking up.

"No, my child. You will never be alone again. Sleep well. Our time is soon coming," said the shadow, walking away.

CHAPTER FOUR: THE CATCH

By Tuesday night, Vanity had been hanging tight with Shante and the word was that she was dancing. And for a Tuesday night, Big Al's was packed like never before. Women and men came out to see Vanity. Watching the line at the door, Big Al smiled. Then Vanity walked up to him and squeezed his ass. He tightened up and looked at her like she was trippin'.

"Oh, Big Al, don't act like you don't like it. I see it all over your face. You like your ass touched and licked. Probably like a little finger action too. You know I can read people." She winked, then continued with her real issue.

"But Big Al let's talk real. What do I get as a star performer?" The confidence her in tone and expression said that she was in control.

"You trippin', but I will break you off a little extra, plus no bar fee. How that sound?" he asked nervously.

"Big Al, don't worry. I got some for you too, and I won't tell no one what you really want me to do. I hear your mind, Al," she said.

"Stop that evil shit," he tried to sound like he was in control, but the way he stepped back from her said otherwise.

Vanity's name was called and she walked off from Big Al and through the crowd as if she ran the place. She knew who they were there for and owned that role. DJ Mega Sounds was bringing it as usual. As Vanity hit the stage, money rained from all directions. She was more than a dancer; she was an entertainer.

As she exited the stage, people hollered for her to check them, but her eyes were on one person. While performing, she'd seen Splack walk in and be seated. She wanted to know if they had a deal. C.W. grabbed her arm and pulled her to him. He'd been drinking and was real aggressive. This didn't scare her though. She gave him a dance and when she turned and looked in C.W.'s eyes, she realized they were hazel like hers. Her heart dropped and she froze in place. C.W. looked back at her confused, then Splack called her. That was enough to break her trance. She made her way over to his table.

"Look Vanity, I believe we can work out our 50/50. Just let me know what area it's in so we can finalize it," Splack said, getting straight to the point.

"It's out on the Southside, almost by Mama Sula," said Vanity, looking back at C.W.

"Okay, cool. That's an area I have power in. Give me the time and day 'cause I need my people to check it out before that day."

"It should be in a few days before the heroin drop, but let me ask you...Who is that guy?" she asked, nodding her head in C.W.'s direction.

"Good. Can I get you in to check security first?"

"There's only one body guard on the property and he moves around with no real schedule. He's always drinking though, so the job easy. I just need it not to look like me or for everybody in the house to be killed," she said.

"Cool. Oh yeah, his name is C.W.," Splack said, smiling like a lottery winner.

As Vanity made her way back to C.W., Splack tapped MannyBo. MannyBo and Bones were off to hit the spot before Vanity knew. Regardless what she said, Splack believed the money was already there. To avoid Vanity backing out or double-crossing them, he ordered MannyBo and Bones to go ahead and hit the house.

***

"Bones, you got the glass cutter and wire cutters right?" MannyBo asked.

"Yeah, man, yeah. Got the acid, heater and the safe buster too," Bones answered.

"Bones, this money. So all that trippin', you can kill."

"Manny, ain't nobody trippin'. Just remember, you ain't my boss. Now let's do this. Cut they throats, bust the safe, and let's live like dons supposed too." Bones had murder in his eyes. MannyBo gave him dap as they parked at a vacant house about a yard down. They cut through the woods in the back and crossed the low section of the fence. They'd checked the alarm system beforehand and, thanks to their inside man at Breaks, Inc., it wasn't in operation. The job would be an easy in and easy out.

Manny checked the perimeter with the night vision, but didn't see a guard. They made their way to the side of the house near two trees. Bones climbed in the windows first. No one anywhere. As they made their way to the back sliding door, Bones held up his hand to stop.

"What?" Manny whispered.

"Smells like a dog or something," Bones answered.

"She said no dogs," MannyBo said. He took it upon himself to keep moving.

He took a crow bar and quietly lifted the sliding door. They made their way in and the smell grew stronger.

"Shit, I smell it too," said MannyBo, taking out a 22 with a silencer.

Bones did the same. They reached the kitchen, Bones looked in the refrigerator but only saw raw chopped meat.

"Damn," he said, closing the refrigerator door.

"Clock," MannyBo reminded Bones. He nodded and they quickened their pace, but in small steps. Not more than three seconds later, Bones put his hand up again.

"What?" MannyBo asked, half nervous, half aggravated.

"Shadow moved."

"You trippin," MannyBo said, pacing towards the next dark room. There were five candles burning on the floor.

"The shadow is the candles," said MannyBo.

Bones shook his head and checked behind them. When Bones turned around, MannyBo was gone.

"Bo," Bones called. No response.

"Bo," called again.

"No time for playing." The shadow moved again.

"Shit, Manny if that's you, stop playing before I shoot the shit out of you." He stepped further in the room and noticed that the candles were in a circle, and inside the circle was MannyBo's head.

"Oh shit!" He tried to run, but tripped over a candle. Made it to the door then a hand grabbed him by his throat.

***

Back at Big Al's, Vanity jumped up as though she sensed something. She ran to the dressing room and put her clothes on. Big Al was right behind her. "What's wrong, Vanity? I said I got you," he pleaded.

"I made good. Just time to go," she said, getting dressed.

"What's wrong, Big Al? You look worried," Splack asked, standing at the bar.

"Nah, I knew fucking with this crazy bitch would be problems. I sensed it from day one this bitch was evil. She evil, you know," said Big Al.

"What happened?" Splack asked. Big Al shrugged and scratched his head.

"She got to go all of a sudden."

"Damn!"

"Shit, who you telling? I need her for business. You just want a dance," said Big Al.

"Nah, we need her all the same," Splack said, holding out his arm to stop

Vanity. The look she gave him muted him mid-sentence.

"So predictable. The pleasure was mine," she said to him, but didn't pause to let him respond. She walked right past him and out the front door. By the time he made it to the door, she had jumped in the car and sped off.

"What the fuck happened? Damn, Manny, call me," Splack said to himself.

"Nardy, look...I need you to try and follow Vanity and see what's going on with her," said Splack.

"Nah, Splack I don't fuck with evil. I told you Grandma said there was an evil spirit around the same day that bitch showed up," said Nardy, Tina's baby daddy.

"What the fuck? All pussy eating bitches are evil to baby daddy," Splack huffed.

"What you mean by that?"

"You heard the girl took Tina out the club the other night after feeling on her. She probably the reason Tina ain't here sweatin' you like usual. You gettin' ate up by a woman and that's the evil Grandma seen," said Splack.

"Man you playing, but if you right, I'ma murk this chick." Nardy climbed in his car.

"She on her way to Old Montgomery, so if you hit the highway, you can catch her." Nardy pulled off, hung up with Splack, and called Tina.

"Tee, where you stayed at the other night?" he asked her.

"Boy, stop playin'. I was with Shante. Why?" she asked. He started to tell her about herself, but shook his head and hung up instead.

"Lying ass. Shante's sister called Terry to come over 'cause Shante wasn't there," he said to himself. Racing down the highway, he could hear his grandmother's words: *The evil is here, baby. Beware. Its form is always vanity to the eyes.*

He exited the highway and eased on down Old Montgomery. He pulled out his phone for more directions. "Yo, Splack. I'm here and I'm not sure why you didn't come. So where you want...hold up...what the fuck? This bitch standing in the street up here," Nardy said, slowing

down. He sat the phone down on the seat, but didn't hang up.

"What's wrong with you?" he rolled down the window and asked her.

"I locked my keys in the car and now I can't even get in the house. What you doing down here anyway?" she asked, smiling.

"I got a powder play back here. You need a ride?" he asked.

"Nah, if you can help me get in the window, I can get the extra keys for the car."

"Alright, but let me run right up here and catch my play and I'll be right back," he said.

"Okay, I'll wait. I don't mind," she said.He pulled off and rode about two streets up and parked. He picked up the phone and

Splack was still holding. "Look, Splack, that bitch scared me. What is up before I go back? I'm not playing. Give me the truth now."

"Yeah, she spooks me too, especially with her standing out in the street like she waiting on you. I heard and I'm glad you left the phone on. When you go back, do the same so I can listen," said Splack.

"You didn't hear me? I ain't going back unless you tell me what's up. I know when I feel a set up," says Nardy.

"Look, we on phones, Nardy and too much too deep already, but look, a lick was involved. Manny and Bones were sent and I haven't heard from them since. And they were in the same area, you feel me? It involved some big people, so if you don't feel her, don't go. It could be a hit 'cause it's blood raw," said Splack.

"Oh, that's so sweet, but unless you bring yo ass down here to talk to me, you won't see baby cuz no more," Vanity said.

"What the fuck you doing?" Splack yelled.

"Nah, what you doing? Trying to cross me out? Your boys on my side for the money and we gon' knock off Nardy, unless you come and agree to stop double crossing," she said.

"Bitch, you playing a gangsta's game. Now you better check yourself before I send a nation of goons down there. Now put my cuz on the phone before—" Dial tone.

"What the fuck?" He dropped the phone in his lap and his chin to his chest. He paused to take a few deep breaths to get his mind together. He had to think of something and fast. When he lifted his head, he spotted Dre in the parking lot.

"Dre, come ride with me. I need to holler at you!" he yelled through the window.

"No problem, fam," said Dre, walking over.

"Look, Dre...You my lil' bro and I need you to check on Mama and give her the numbers on this paper. She'll know what they for. I gotta handle something real quick," said Splack.

"Bro, you don't sound right," said Dre.

"Nah, it's all good, just a G being a G. Now get out and handle that. I'll hit you in a few." Splack turned on Tupac's "Hail Mary" as he slipped on his vest and pulled the AR out the case. The smoke from the blunt was so heavy it just hovered like a thick cloud in Splack's face, moving with the music. As Splack passed through the traffic, it was like he was the only one moving.

"God, only you can save me now," Splack prayed as he turned off to head down Old Montgomery. He rode through the area, looking for the spot Nardy said that he'd parked at. It didn't take long to find his car. Splack hopped out like a special force unit. Sitting in the car was Nardy and Vanity, aiming a 45 to his head.

"Now look, I thought you would bitch up and get scared and not come and I would have had to kill this beautiful baby boy," said Vanity.

"Look, Vanity, the game you playing is about to cost you," warned Splack.

She hit Nardy with the tip of the gun and he got quiet. "Look, you tried to cross me. You better hope that this has not messed me up on this lick. Now I make the calls and I pick the people. I'm not sure what happened to your people, but the bosses here said they were upset, mentioning a burglar. It's my call! You got me?"

"Bitch, what make you think that you got the power like that?" Splack asked.

"'Cause all I have to do is tell the Boss that I know who followed me here and tried to commit the robbery and they will do the rest. That being said, I also know when the package is dropped off and where to find the money. Plus, I'm holding the gun. Now how does that sound?" She punctuated her question with a smile.

"Alright, explain it out," Splack reasoned.

"I felt like your boy C.W. was more trustworthy, so that's who I want on this job. His word is bond. Now the package is dropped off and only stays for one day and must be timed after the delivery. For three hours, there is only one guard, then everyone returns and that can mean 10 to 20 people. I so believe his so-called mistake has to stop." She dropped the gun from Nardy's head and kissed him on the spot.

"Kill the bitch, Cuz. She lethal," says Nardy.

"Be easy, Cuz. She just a real gangster chick. Anyway, you just mad 'cause she caught you slipping," said Splack.

"Nah, Splack...She caught you slipping and everyone gonna pay for underestimating this evil fuck," Nardy said, cranking up his car. Vanity got out of the car and stood laughing in the headlights before disappearing behind the tree line.

"Splack, you see how she move. She evil. Ain't no way she ran down here from the

house and put the pistol on me so quietly. Just check yourself. This real major league," Nardy said as he backed out. Splack jumped back in his Tahoe and pulled out behind Nardy.

"What da fuck happen to MannyBo and Bones? This crazy. Now I got to get fucking loose wire C.W. and his fucking partner, Skeeta," Splack complained to himself as he turned to get back on the highway.

CHAPTER FIVE: SHADOW REVEALED

Early Wednesday morning, Splack was up heading to Sandfly, another Southside Neighborhood, to talk to C.W. and Skeeta.

"Cee, what's up? I hope you up. I need you to ride with me," said Splack."Yeah, I'm up. Just got through feeding the dogs. Come on, I'll ride," said C.W. "Cool, I'll be pullin' up in five minutes," said Splack."Hey Skeeta, Splack coming through in a few. Hurry up and roll up so we can smoke

first," said C.W.

"Man, I been rolled. Just waiting on you," said Skeeta as he fired up the blunt. As C.W. walked over to the shed, Splack pulled up. Skeeta handed C.W. the blunt and then took the dog food into the shed.

"Damn, Splack you was right round the corner," said C.W.

"Yeah, but so is a nice payday," said Splack in a conman's voice.

"Well if we can smoke in the ride, I'm ready, but if not, let me finish with Skeeta," said C.W.

"Nah, Skeeta cool, and we can ride and smoke. I got two rolled up already," said Splack.

"Now this must be a big payday."

"Hop in and I'll explain."C.W. and Skeeta both got in and Splack pulled off.

"We gonna ride out to the beach. I know a breakfast spot we can catch there. So yeah, this the big one, a life changer. I figure you two can get $500,000 apiece. Is that good?" asked Splack.

"Sounds good, but life just ain't that easy, Splack. If we getting that, you getting triple, at least. Now these type of licks don't just fall in your lap by accident. So first question is who involved 'cause the double-cross somewhere," asked C.W. as he slowly pulled the blunt.

"See, my man C.W. He sharp like a razor and his words...they like knowledge," said Skeeta.

"Yeah, Yeah, Skeeta. Look, C.W, it's a hit on the mob, an Italian boss living in our area and got major things coming in and out. So happen, the trick Vanity been working him. He got a tender dick and been pillow talking. She just want her cut and for us to kill him so he can't track her," explained Splack.

"Shit, that's all you had to say. Now do you trust this Vanity?"

"Well, she is lethal, but that way I know her part is good," said Splack, looking away.

"Splack, your head movement says you are unsure on that. Look, this ain't no game. This is life. So tell me, does she have a reason to cross you?" asked C.W.

"Man, C.W., you sharp. You checked that nigga head movement. Shit, I think the bitch fine, but she is creepy too. But I would suck that—"

"—Shut up, Skeeta," Splack said, cutting him off.

"Nah, she down. I done tapped that and I paid very well. Look, I'm splitting my cut with little Nardy. So that's the only other one," said Splack as he reached for the blunt.

"Alright, Splack. Word is bond. So when we begin planning this out?" asked C.W.

"What you mean?" asked Splack.

"Look, Splack...You called me and I am a professional at this. So first we put a wire and camera on the girl Vanity, so we can see inside and map the house out. Then we know our timing and exit. Nothing like going into a place and not knowing how to get out if something happen. So call the chick, tell her what she got to do, then I'll bring the equipment. That's not a problem is it?" asked C.W.

"Alright, I'll tell her, but she be tripping sometimes," said Splack.

"Shit, *shit*," yelled Skeeta.

"What the fuck wrong with you?" asked C.W.

"I dropped the dam blunt on this new ass Coogi."

As they parked, Splack called Vanity. "Look Van, your boy you chose, he got his own way of doing things. So you may need to meet us for lunch at Island Breeze, okay?"

"I can handle that, but if you try anything funny, I will shoot you," she said.

"Cool, see you at about 12:30."

"Damn, we gonna have lunch with that fine ass bitch? Why you ain't hotel, motel, holiday end, so I can bend her big ole ass over and be her best friend? Oh, boy my dick hard already thinking 'bout that evil eyed bitch."

"Man, Skeeta stay focused. This business," said Splack.

"Man, this ain't no corporate job. All we know in these streets is business and pleasure. What else is there? The shit you do either put you in prison for hundred years or you get murked in the process. So nah, Negro. I am down, but my dick hard," Skeeta said as he pimps to the restaurant door.

"He right, Skeeta. This the mafia and this chick with them, meaning she ain't nothing to take lightly," said C.W.

"Now if y'all gonna make this some scary shit, don't tell me. You know me. Give me a choppa and I'll cut loose 'cause my ass ain't with no mob boss cutting me up in little pieces and shit," says Skeeta.

"Hold that down, Skee. We in the restaurant now," said Splack.

"That's what I'm saying. You two hold that shit down 'cause I don't want to hear it either," said Skeeta.

"Table for three?" asked the host.

"Yes, that will be fine," Splack answered.

"Well, I know you boys won't leave me out." Vanity said as she taps Splack on the shoulder.

"What the fuck? Oh shit, I know this bitch ain't just pop out of thin air," said Skeeta looking scared as he stares her up and down and looks around to see where she came from.

"So will it be four instead?" the host asked.

"Yes," answered C.W. as he looked around outside.

"Follow me please," she said, leading them to their table.

"What's wrong, Splack? You've been following me. Why can't I follow you to see what you're up to?" She winked at him.

"I understand, but you may spook our help," said Splack as he watched C.W. come back to the table.

"Why the fuck you creeping on us like you the police," asked C.W.

"Thank you, C.W. 'cause my dick was hard until this bitch scared me," said Skeeta like he was about to cry.

"Y'all done talked about the mafia and cutting me up and now this bitch creep up on us like this? Lord, this shit too deep. Why y'all scare me like that? My dick won't even get hard and her titties right there talking me, begging me to kiss 'em."

Both Splack and C.W. told him to shut up.

"Chill, Skeeta. Let her talk for a moment," C.W. added, staring Vanity down. Not like a man would stare at a woman, but in the way that a detective would stare at a suspect.

"Well I did that 'cause I don't want to get crossed out either and Splack be having people follow me too. So I felt that a dose of his own medicine was good for him," Vanity pleaded.

"Damn, Splack. You terrorizing the girl. Come here and let me hug you. I'm sorry he like that. He just crazy. Come on, let me please hug you," said Skeeta with his arms outstretched.

"Stop, Skeeta. So Vanity and Splack been playing this game for a minute. I don't play games. It's just business and if you forget that I will blow your head off myself. You got me?" C.W. asked her, still staring her down.

"Under different circumstances, I would have probably kissed you. But I do understand. Oh, and Skeeta please give me a hug," she said laughing.

Skeeta jumped up so fast he spilled his water. He gave her a hug and a little titty grab.

"Oh, under different circumstances I would've stripped butt naked and told you I love you, but they may kick us out for that, so can we plan for maybe tonight," Skeeta suggested, looking serious.

"Skeeta, only if you brought C.W., but I think he scared of me. But after all of this is over, I will give you a special dance, okay?"

"Are you ready to place your orders?" the waitress asked.

Everybody ordered and as they ate lunch, Skeeta tried to feel on Vanity every five minutes. As C.W. explained how he needed her to put the camera on her purse so he could map out the house, she greed. Splack looked confused considering how hard she'd been tripping about being in control of things.

"Well can I sit in the truck with you guys and smoke one 'cause I know you got one rolled already?" Vanity asked as they walked back to their cars.

"Shit yeah, you can sit in the back on my lap," said Skeeta.

"Why I got to sit on your lap? It's only three of you."

"It will help you get higher and higher the longer you sit there," Skeeta tried to convince her.

"Boy, you crazy," said C.W.

"Nah, we will break it in half. I got to go get my sister. She got class soon and I have to take her," said C.W.

"Oh, you have a sister. What's her name?" asked Vanity.

"Her name is opposite of yours. It's Divine," said C.W. as he sat down in the truck. Splack broke the blunt in half and handed it to her.

"I'll see you at 4:00, C.W. for the hook up. Mama Sula's right?" Vanity said walking off, leaving Splack standing there holding the blunt.

"Why y'all do me like that? She was going to sit on my lap. But C.W like Nah we break it in half. Just hate on my chance to romance. When I get some real money, I'm going to buy some exotic pussy, Lord," said Skeeta, watching Vanity get in her car.

"This C.W. may be just what I really need," Vanity said to herself as she rode off.

C.W. gets a call, "Look, big bro. I need to be on time. So are you nearby 'cause if you ain't, I will call someone else?"

"I'll be there in a few minutes. Go ahead and take your stuff to the car," said C.W.

"Alright, I called early so you wouldn't forget me," said Divine.

"Divine, I can't forget you when you call me every hour on the hour. Plus, you the only thing I really love. I'll see you in a minute," says C.W.

"Thanks, Bro. It's nice to hear that. I made you something anyways," she teased.

"The famous pecan pie," she said before hanging up.

"Damn, Mister Sentimental, and you trippin' about me wanting a hug from a dollar? Yeah, a dollar. Not a dime, not a quarter, but a damn dollar. Let me be sentimental sometimes. I ain't got no damn sister to balance me out," said Skeeta.

"Skeeta, you crazy. But I feel yah. She is fine. But too damn slick though. I hate a chick you can't read," said C.W.

"Well you told her we had a camera, but you didn't tell her it was a mic too. So maybe it will catch something she don't want us to hear," said Skeeta.

"I thought you missed that," said C.W., smiling.

"Man, C.W. I listen real good, 'specially when this scary shit going on. Mafia and cutting you up in the basement shit. I'm gon' know my way out that damn house," said Skeeta.

"So once you map the house, we'll be ready, right?" Splack asked with thoughts of MannyBo and Bones disappearing.

"Man, C.W. is this man slow or what? What the fuck you think we just rookies—?" Skeeta started.

"Damn, man!" Skeeta said, shaking his head.

Splack turned up Tupac's "Who do you believe in," and everyone got quiet and just rode listening. As they pulled up in the yard, Divine stood, waiting with her locks wrapped, sporting an Angela Davis t-shirt and a wrap skirt looking like a goddess. Divine was truly what you called a conscious black woman, and she rode C.W. everyday about it. What most people didn't know was that C.W. stood for Conscious Wisdom. Yes, his mother had named him Conscious and her Divine. C.W was older than Divine, but somehow she played the mother role.

"Hello, Skeeta. Hello, Splack," Divine greeted them as C.W. and Skeeta got out of Splack's truck.

"Splack, I'll call later," said C.W. as he closed the truck door. Splack lightly tapped the horn.

"Divine, why my hair won't grow like yours?" joked Skeeta.

"You need to stop eating *dead flesh*," she answered, climbing into C.W.'s candy green Porsche truck. She looked as regal as its all-white interior. C.W. hit the start button and the UGK blared through the speaker.

"Please cut that off and play your Nas and Damian Marley instead," she said.

"Use the remote. It's the fifth CD," said Skeeta like the truck was his.

"Look Skeeta, we make this lick and we movin'," said C.W. as he handed Skeeta his bag of gadgets from out the garage.

"C.W., I need to talk to you privately later too. So before you get involved in anything, come see me. I have something to tell you, okay?" Though her voice was soft, there was a push of authority behind it.

"Alright, Divine. I know you eavesdropping on me and Skeeta conversation, but it's all good."

"Nah, C.W. it don't have nothing to do with your conversation. I just need to talk to you as I always do."

"I don't know, Divine. Why you two act like I am not around every day? I know your little root lady ass been reading for him and you got something. So please don't shit round the bush 'cause of me. I tell his ass he need to check what Root Mama say. Now all that said, C.W. answer your sister, please," said Skeeta.

Both Divine and C.W. laughed, amazed at Skeeta. "I don't know why y'all laughing at me. I be with you two everyday. Feeding these stink dogs. Washing this loud color ass car and helping you," he said, poking Divine's shoulder, "with your funny root garden. So please act like I am family at some point. Cause your Mama C.W., Divine...R.I.P I am sorry, but I must say. Raise me too," said Skeeta as he sat upright.

"You right, Skeeta. I don't know why I do that. It's really 'cause C.W. act like he don't want people to know how I think. So Skeeta I'm sorry. You are family. Love you," she said before turning around to rub his head.

"Lord, I'm gonna cry. I ask for a sister to be sentimental with after C.W. wouldn't let me get any, and you gave her to me. My first prayer has come true. This a special day," said Skeeta like he was about to cry.

"This dude here. He is family and yes, Divine, I will check with you first," said C.W.

"Okay, now before you pull up to the school, remember to turn the music down," she said, back in mother-mode. As they pulled into Vo-Tech, several girls were sweating the truck as they stopped to let Divine out. Skeeta got out the back seat to get in the front.

"Hey Divine, thank you," Skeeta said. Divine smiled back at him.

"You trying to flirt with my sister?" C.W. joked.

"Shit, to get Divine, you got to stop combing your hair and eat celery sticks all day. That's just too much pressure for the average man. That ain't even including all those books I'd have to read. Man, she beautiful, but I like simple minds."

"I'm just messing with you," said C.W. as he turned the U.G.K. up loud again. C.W. phone rings, but he doesn't hear it because of the music. As he rides and smokes to kill time, Splack is pacing in his yard.

"Cee, look like you got a missed call," Skeeta said, looking down at C.W.'s phone.

"See who is it," said C.W.

"It's a 305 number with no name," said Skeeta.

"Damn, that's Splack. Call it back," said C.W. as he reaches for the phone. Skeeta hits call and hands C.W. the phone.

"Where you at? She called. We got to do the mapping now. It comes tonight. You ready? 'Cause I'm in your yard,"

"We'll be there in 10 minutes. Call her back, but not to my yard. We'll meet you at Walmart parking lot."

He looked at Skeeta and shook his head."Alright, 10 to 15, Walmart," Splack confirmed.

"Damn, you ain't talk to Divine yet?" asked Skeeta.

"Man, Skeeta this the streets. That's why I didn't want her saying that in front of you. Just as I thought, you'll start thinking you need that and end up losing your edge," said C.W.

"You can say what you want, but every trip we made and before every lick, you checked with her. So all bullshit aside, you need to call her," said Skeeta.

"Man, let's just map and I'll talk to her later."

When they pulled into Walmart's parking lot, Vanity was standing there with Shante talking.

"Damn nosey ass Shante," said Skeeta.

"What the fuck she doing with her right now?" asked C.W.

"Shante only gonna think a nigga trying to fuck. So pull up by her and I'll do me." C.W. rolled up on Vanity and Shante real slow.

"Girl, you see how we rolling. Just come sit on my lap one time for all those dollars I slung at your pretty ass the other night," said Skeeta in his hood pimp mode.

"Hold on, Shante," said Vanity as she opened the door and sat on Skeeta's lap.

"Boy you kinda big. I am getting higher. Give me the piece so we can do this. I'm going to drop Shante in a few," Vanity said, grinding on Skeeta.

"Just place it on your purse's latch and keep your arm off it so I can see. After a complete tour, come out and I'll let you know if we got what we need," said C.W. as he eyeing her. Vanity grabbed the gadget and placed it on her purse. She grabbed Skeeta's dick as she got out of the car.

"Boy, you strapped," said Vanity with smile.

"He may be strapped, but he only last a second," said Shante.

"You hating 'cause I never came back for that raggedy Ann," said Skeeta in response.

"Damn, Skeeta, you creep with Shante?" asked C.W. as he pulled off.

"Man, don't tell no one. I was drunk and she raped me," said Skeeta in his crybaby mode. C.W.'s phone rung.

"What?"

"Did it go?" asked Splack.

"You know. See you in Mama Sula's yard," said C.W. as he hung the phone up.

"Skeeta, turn the volume on the mic up. Let's hear the ladies lies," said C.W.

"Oh shit, I forgot about that!" Skeeta pulled the laptop out and logged in.

"That Skeeta, he really got some meat. But girl, he will fall in love in a second. I thought we could creep, but on the first night, he said I love you. It blew the shit out of me," said Shante.

"She lying, man. I'm telling you," Skeeta defended himself.

"Yeah, but he really sweeter than the others," said Vanity.

"I like him, but I don't want no man. The minute a freaky bitch get him, he gonna say I love you. I need to know my man gonna be strong and at least come home afterwards," said Shante.

"What about C.W.? He a mystery. I can't even feel him out," said Vanity.

"Well, he a different breed, and that's all I can say about him. That damn sister of his may read me and I don't need no roots on me."

"What you mean by that?" asked Vanity.

"Well, they say his sister put roots on him to keep women away who mean him no good, but that just stories."

"Is his sister that powerful?"

"Girl, you sound like you believe in that stuff. But nah, his sister younger than him and she in college. People just be trippin'. I think Skeeta started the rumor, myself," said Shante. Skeeta shook his head.

"Man, I'm telling you. She lying again. I don't know why this witch lying on me. Damn, Shante stop lying on me." He yelled at the laptop as if she could hear him.

"What if I told you I do believe in those things, and that I have seen people who are really powerful?"

"Bitch, now you trippin' and that kind of talk scares me. Come on and drop me off and go handle your business. Vanity, you need to find your soul 'cause it's lost out here in the world," warned Shante.

"I'm trying to, Shante. Believe me, I'm trying." Vanity pulled up Shante's sister's apartment behind Hesse Elementary.

"Thank you for the ride, Vanity, and remember life is not all streets," said Shante as she got out.

"Peace," said Vanity as she pulled off.

As she got back on the road, her phone rung. "Hello, sir. No, I have not seen her. But he is present. I will separate them all. No, I have no one with me now. I am sure. The gift...I know, for me and for her. No, I don't know why you sense a presence. Okay, I will see you in a few minutes," she said.

"How the fuck he feel us, or am I tripping?" asked Skeeta.

"Nah, that's just a man trying to see if his girl cheating. He don't feel no one, he just fronting to scare her. I did that one before too just to see if she was by herself," said C.W. like he was reassuring himself.

"Yeah, that's it, but I felt like the muthafucker was looking at me right then. She talkin' 'bout roots and powerful people. See, I don't miss shit."

C.W. lifted his hand for Skeeta to be quiet as they pulled into Mama Sula's yard. He connected an auxiliary cord from the laptop to the radio so they could hear better.

"Come in, my dear. We have only have one more step for you and... Wait, I feel the eyes of souls. Go to the room. I will see you soon, my child. Oh, Eve, did you tell me everything?" asked an elderly man's voice. Unmistakably, it was the voice of the baron.

"Yes, my Lord Dracon. I have," answered Vanity like a child in fear.

"*Damn!* Who this dude with a hoody robe on, acting like Hugh Hefner?"

"Be quiet, Skeeta. I'm trying to hear if it's only him. If it's just that old

Italian, we can beat his ass. But he said some shit like he thinks she lying. What he means by that is confusing," said C.W.

"Damn, the house dark and gloomy," said Skeeta. Someone hit the car window and they both reached for their guns.

"Man, you'll fuck around and get shot playing like that," said Skeeta as he opened the door for Splack to talk.

"You two act like you seen a damn ghost," said Splack.

"Nah, but Vanity stay with hoody man," said C.W., pointing at the laptop.

"Is that moaning?" asked Splack.

"Turn it up, Skeeta," said C.W.

"You trippin.' The man is an Italian boss. You think she the only freak he know? That's probably the second playboy mansion," said Skeeta, turning the volume up on the laptop.

"Look where she walking. It's an office look like. She keeps pointing the purse to the wall with the lower picture. That must be the safe area. Look by the shelf. The safe right there. Damn, this bitch good. Look at that picture. It's an angel with a sword in its heart. That is a really dark house," said C.W.

"Where she going now? Looks like the bathroom. Yep. Now she knows we watching."

"Well one thing, I am not going to stop 'cause of you two. This my time, and I wish I could be alone. Oh, baby take it all off. That's it. Yes, that's it. Now she is really setting it out. Please turn the steam down," Skeeta said, damn near moaning himself.

"Wait, she writing on the mirror. It's a message for us. I CAN...No, it's: I CAN'T LEAVE BACK OUT. Damn, she can't leave, back out. So that means, we got to go tonight with her there," said C.W.

"Man, she got to get out 'cause in the dark I be done shot her pretty ass. You know she like to sneak up on people," said Skeeta.

"What you think, Splack?" asked C.W."I think she don't want to spook him no more than necessary," said Splack.

"I guess it's a go. We'll watch for her to give us the go, and then we'll strike. I guess we need to go change vehicles and clothes now. Look, I need you Splack to get ready. This is a three-person job now," said C.W.

"Man, I am clumsy fingers, slow on the trigger. I just do numbers. Plus, this work out my league," reasoned Splack.

"This your job. You coming on this or no?" asked C.W.

"Okay, but keep my job simple," said Splack.

C.W. pulled off and headed to Pinpoint. He had an old LTD covered in plastic tarp in his auntie's yard. They all got a Dickie suit out the truck, gloves, and plastic covering for their shoes. C.W. grabbed what he called the doctor's bag, and they pulled back around to Mama Sula's yard. The LTD had such dark tint, no one could see inside. As they watched Vanity get dressed and walk around her room, they waited patiently for a sign. They had left all phones in the other car, so no one would accidently drop one at the scene.

"Did you see her tattoo? It was a unicorn with wings, but the devil was riding it. Now that was a serious piece," said Skeeta.

"What did you say it was?" asked C.W.

"A unicorn with wings and the devil riding it," repeated Skeeta.

"There's buddy. What the fuck is he doing with that damn monk robe on? There's the opening of the safe. This is a big safe. That looks like a gold bar in there too. She pointing the purse. Perfect," said Splack, nodding.

"Yeah, too damn perfect, seems," said C.W.

"Listen, it is time make the call," said the Italian.

"I have, my Lord. The delivery has arrived and the package will be prepared for pick up in seven hours," said Vanity as she lit a candle.He then begins to speak a language no one could understand.

"What the hell are they doing?" asked Splack.

"It looks like he doing some kind of ritual, but I can't tell," said C.W. as they pulled off to head to the house.

"Oh my God, look at his eyes. They're all white. Is that the light of the camera? He looks like he is 80 years old. Look at the tattoo on his head," said Skeeta.

"It's a symbol called the blade of death. It represents the Fallen Ones' Order, who secretly rule this world. But many bikers and gangs took those symbols. My sister points 'em out all the time," said C.W. as he parked and put on his gloves.

"Side door entrance. Back route to bedroom. Back track and circle to safe room. Just like we went over," instructed C.W. as he pulled down his mask. They all got out and move the back route along the fence to the back door area.

CHAPTER SIX: ENTRANCE

The back door was opened with a curtain hanging like a veil. C.W. tapped it to peep in.

"Clear," he said then waved them to follow him inside. Skeeta nudged C.W. and pointed to his nose. C.W. nodded his head. The scent of a dog or some type of animal was heavy in the air. The house had a candle lit in almost every corner. Following the plan, they came to a hallway where several daggers and swords hung on the wall like collector's prize. Skeeta grabbed the gold one. C.W. shook his head then grabbed the silver one with a black stone on the tip of the handle. They placed the dagger in their belts. Splack tapped C.W. and pointed down at the water they were stepping in. C.W. aimed the flashlight on the floor and saw that it wasn't water. It was blood.

"Ohhhhhhh," said Skeeta.

C.W. shook his head to quiet him back down. Splack didn't see, so he looked up confused.

"Straps," C.W. whispered as he pulled out an extended clip Max-10. Skeeta immediately pulled his mini AR off of his back. Splack followed suit. C.W. raised his hand as approached a room with light seeping from the door. Skeeta took a deep breath and shook his head, trying to shake the bad feeling that washed over him.

Back at the house, Divine paced back and forth, feeling the danger that C.W. was in.

"Where are you at, Bro? Please answer your phone," she whined. She leaned her head against the nearest wall to take a few deep breaths. She needed to think rationally, not emotionally. Then it clicked. She went into her meditation room and made a circle on the floor with sage and lit 12 candles and myrrh incense. She poured a libation into a bowl and brought it to the middle of the circle with her. Seated in the center of the circle, she took a small silver dagger and cut her hand just enough to release three drops of blood. As they dripped into the bowl, she chanted a prayer of protection. As she did so, the flames of the candle began to flicker violently. The candles at the mob boss's house did the same. C.W. noticed first and knew exactly what was happening. Divine had told him the elements will speak.

"Let's leave. It's not right," he said, backing up.

"No, too close," said Splack.

"Skeeta, let's go," said C.W.

"There's a 100 keys of heroin and five mill in cash," Splack reminded them.

"Man, that...," Skeeta started, shaking his head.

C.W. continued backing up slowly.

"Even split," Splack bargained.

"Cee," Skeeta pleaded.C.W. just shook his head. All of a sudden, the candles went out. A cold breeze followed.

A door opened and the light was blindingly bright. They shielded their eyes, but kept looking to see what was going on. Vanity walked out completely nude and waved them to hurry inside.

"Come, Come, Come," she said standing in the doorway. Splack stepped forward, then C.W. pulled his shoulder back. Splack shook himself out of C.W.'s grip and Skeeta followed him toward the room.

"No, Skee," C.W. warned.

"I'm just looking, Cee," Skeeta answered.She walked back inside of the room and the light went out. Skeeta stopped and looked back at C.W.

Splack stepped in the room. The light came back on all of a sudden. Skeeta

shrugged and walked closer to the door.

"Let's go, Skee" C.W. pleaded with him.Before Skeeta could consider changing his mind, Vanity yanked him into the room. C.W. raised the Mac-10 to firing mode and charged the door. Once in, total darkness took over again.

"Skee," C.W. called out, spinning around. He spots the shadows lurking and thinks how they've been set up. He squeezed the trigger trying to hit one of the moving shadows. As the fire shot from C.W.'s gun, it froze mid-air. He was knocked to the floor and the gun flew from his hand. What shook him most is that it wasn't a person who'd pushed him down, but rather a force of some sort.

"Skeeta, where are you?" yelled C.W., standing to his feet. Looking around, he sees Splack's head in the middle of the floor circled with candles.

"Oh shit!" C.W. raced to pick up his gun. Vanity kicked it away. The old, white man from the video appeared behind her.

"Vanity, what you doing?" asked C.W.

"Making an offering for life," she answered coldly.The elderly man began chanting in a foreign language. A great light opened like a door above the circle. The same force that'd knocked C.W. down grabbed his legs and lifted him to the circle. He fought to free himself, but to no avail. The elderly man fully emerged into the room and removed his hood. The tattoo on his head seemed to be leaking blood.

"I am the blade of death, but soon your blood will bring fire to the power of my lord," he said. Just as Skeeta had pointed out in the video, his eyes were pure white, absent of pupils. He raised the blade above his head.

"The blood of the male and the blood of the female, the son and daughter..."

C.W. grabbed the dagger out of his belt and stabbed the man in the head. He jumped up and went straight for his gun. Vanity jumped back and then disappeared into what looked to be a secret door. C.W. didn't hesitate to shoot. Several more white men, looking just like the first, came at him. As he shot at them, his bullets froze in the air as if he were in the middle of the damn Matrix. One of them got close enough to him to rip the vest from his chest. C.W. stabbed his hand with the dagger to free himself. He ran to the other side of the room. They surrounded him like lions closing in on a gazelle. Just as back hit a wall and he'd began to accept his fate, he heard his sister's words: *"Remember Cee, they use the elements to exist on this plane. You must use it against them to take their power."* He began slicing candles and breaking up the circle of power. The room went totally dark.

"Oh, Divine...I'm sorry."

"Be strong, brother. They sense fear. They are circling you still. You have trapped them on this plane. The gun will work now that their field is broken. Now that your mind has opened to hear me, I know it is time. Search the room for a veil. There must be a window. Move slow."

"I'm going crazy," said C.W. He started shooting the walls.

"Light. The window...," he said just as he was being charged by what looked to be a half man, half dog.

"Oh, shit!" he yelled, turning to shoot it. It turned and ran the other way.

C.W. shot the window before jumping out of it. He crashed through the window and landed on the ground. Shards of glass struck him in the leg and back. Testosterone pumping, he didn't even feel it. He got up and ran towards the fence. That's when the pain hit him. Instead of hopping the fence, he easily climbed his way over. He looked back and saw Vanity peering down at him from the broken window. Beside her was another robed man holding Skeeta, who was tied up. He limped his way back to the car and sped off, crying. Once in his aunt's yard, he switches cars and pulls out his cellphone. There were 27 missed calls from Divine.

"Divine, I am so sorry. I know, I know you told me. But listen it is a long story. Pack up what you can and be ready. We got to leave."

"Cee, are you alright? I'm waiting," she said.As C.W. raced to his house, his phone rung.

"Hello," he answered, still trying to catch his breath.

"Nooo, Nooo, pleeease!" yelled Skeeta, and then the phone hung up.

"Oh shit, Skeeta." He pulled into his front yard, put the car in park, laid his head on the steering wheel, and cried. Divine rushed out to him.

"Divine...we...I. I can't explain. We just got to go," he said with tears in his eyes.

"Conscious, I know. I saw and spoke to you. Come with me," she said in the voice of mother comforting her child.Divine had to help him out of the truck and into the house. She sat him down and began cutting his pant legs off to remove the glass. She already had the first aid kit ready, including peroxide and sewing material to stitch him up.

"How did you—"

She placed a finger over his mouth. "Cee, you must trust me and yourself right now. Life has many dimensions. For this word is not flat lined. It's not dead. It has dimensions, many sides, but most of us are only aware of one side. You have just witnessed another side. What you previously thought was evil and good was only a one-sided view."

"But—"

She shook her head to silence him, then continued. "There are only those who know and those who don't. But in the middle are those who have chosen to rule through knowledge of truth in life. But they have done so by destroying others, so their power is life force of other people. You call them vampires. They have been here for many ages, since the great meteorite shower. Divine beings who became fiend spirits on this plane. They were the ones who caused the electromagnetic field of this plane to change by spiritual unbalance, causing the meteorite shower. When the sudden destruction of their so-called physical body would not let go of their physical desire, they became stuck in between the planes of physical and astral.

She knotted the thread as she explained, "So they waited ages until they could attack on to bodies and consume their life force. Remember the story I told you about how there came to be a race wars from the ones who got caught in the meteorite shower and fled to the cave, eventually becoming cavemen, and later the Caucasian race?"

"Yeah, I remember, but Divine we need to go," C.W. said trying to stand up.

"Listen now. Mama wanted you to understand," she said. He saw the tears in her eyes and sat back down.

"Divine, Mama died giving birth to you. How do you know what she wanted me to know?"

Before their father died, he gave Divine their mother's diary. She placed it on the table to better introduce what she had to tell him. "Dad gave me this before he died. He only drank 'cause he was sad about Mom. He said she would come and talk to him, and people thought he was crazy. I did too until she came to me." She opened the diary.

"Read," she ordered.

"It is my destiny, but I accept it for I know the time grows near. Oh, Divine, Oh Conscious, I know the day will come when you both will read together trying to understand the battle before you. Yes, my children, a battle for control, which is what our Family Order has protected for ages. It is the Wheel of Destiny. This is the controlling fate of this world as we know it. It is a Celestial Battle for control. Divine, if you have followed my instruction, you should be ready to complete your priestess position. Conscious, I know the world would not allow you to see clearly, so I left several books and people to guide you.

After the Spirits of those caught in the in-between gained power over the cavemen, they found that melanin in blood made them stronger and was a gateway allowing them form. They also began to fight with those who had lost their spiritual dominion on this plane. They did this because they need man to operate in a lower nature so they could feed off their energy, but the Ancient Ones who had not lost their Spiritual dominion was teaching all how to rise above the fallen lower nature. This was the battle, for the astral plane is a wheel. And unless they can charge it with a force for them to rule, their time will run out. But if they could gain real power in the Astral realms of this world, they can take over.

Now this is where we come in. Once it was realized the battle at hand, a sacred priesthood was created to protect the Wheel of destiny, for certain points astrologically marked what is deemed star-gates in which they can bring in ancient armies of their force and several Ancient ones of their original fallen, especially the androgynous one of no name. From Egypt came under Ahmoses. I am Empress Nefatari, the divine decree that the sacred right would move to the lands of the West, for the final battle would be fought there. The seven scared vessels of the Temple were sent. But these were not just any old temple vessels. These where sacred Mothers. They are the Oracles of Kings and Mothers of Emperors and Empresses. They were sent here and became the seven sacred tribes of the Americas.

Why are they the scared vessels? Because when the priestess produces a son, that son is made to marry another priestess daughter. Once the priestess becomes pregnant with a daughter, she must transcend this plane or, as some see it, she must die. But this is only the key to the

wheel. For they now have power. Divine, I am going in labor now. Both of you, know I am always with you. I love you." C.W. refolded the letter and placed it back on the table as he began to cry.

"Cee, Mama was a priestess. When I found out, I went to Mama Sula 'cause I figured she'd know. She took me to Queen Mother Yamasee, who said the wheel was turning. So I studied everything, and as I did, I learned to hear and see Mama. Why you think I grew my locks?" she asked as she finished wrapping her brother's leg.

"So all we need to do is go and live long and have babies? Let's go." He picked up his keys.

"No, Cee. Didn't you pay attention? This is our battle. They are trying to open a gate and take over. If they do, where you gonna run then?" She was obviously irritated.

"Let's just run until then. I'll learn more along the way," he said, limping away to pack a bag.

"Cee, you a son of a priestess called one of the Golden Queen Mothers. They need your blood to do what they want. They not going to let us run. They came here for us. Plus, I been doing research and I don't know if they got the other Golden Queen Mothers children yet. Mama said there are seven who guard the way. They been attacking them, so the seven Golden Queen Mothers were in the year about 1490 made a secret even amongst the people of the tribes in fear someone would kill them. They initiated all the Women as one of the Sacred Seven. That is how I was able to finish the Rites of Passage, because they were preserved through secrecy all these years. But Cee, I think we're the last ones," she said, crying.

"Oh, baby girl. I am sorry. You been carrying this weight for so long time. I just don't know what to do. I'm scared and I know only one thing, Divine. I don't want nothing to happen to you. When I see you, I see Mama, and I know we are different, but I am just unsure if I got any of Mama's gifts like you. You've always been my hero, even though I never said it. I love your power to be different and stay divine. But Divine." He took a deep breath.

"I saw Splack's head on the floor and blood all through that house and I felt death grab me, and...Skeeta...damn, they had Skeeta and they called me so I could hear him scream." He dropped the bag and sat back down.

"Cee, we got to try to save Skeeta. That's why they called you to use him to... I'm not sure what they truly want but we must still save Skeeta", says Divine as she tries to hold her tears from falling.

C.W grabbed his sister by her shoulders. "Divine, Skeeta dead and we have to leave. That's just that. I have to protect you, especially if you the last of the seven."

She responded by picking up her board and cowrie shells. She went back to her meditation room and let a black candle.

"Erzulie Danballah," she chanted in an unknown tongue.

C.W spent his time packing their belongings and taking it to the truck, carrying an AK-47 strapped to him. As he turned to get more stuff, Divine met him at the door. "Cee, Skeeta is not dead. His force is still on this plane, but he is suffering. Mama told me so."

"Divine, my mind made up. We can't afford to lose you," he answered her.

"Cee, he is our family, remember?"

"You right, Divine. So what you want me to do?" He felt bad about it, but really didn't know what else to do.

"We can do this, C.W, but you must trust that there are forces on your side to help us win. Just as you heard me before, keep listening. What is that in your belt?" she asked. "A dagger I grabbed off the wall." He handed it to Divine.

"Damn, the blade of Isis with the Black Eye of Ra. This is a really powerful tool. This means that a leader is here. This is very ancient dagger. Here, keep it. It'll help you. The stone is power to those who can hold the staff of Tehuti. But in my studies, I found the staff of Tehuti to be an opening of the Third Eye, or the Kundalini force. Remember the meditation class we took together when we were young? Those will be your weapons in this battle. Here's a medicine bag. A sprinkle around you will protect you for maybe an hour or so. I honestly don't know how powerful they are." She handed him a clear stone.

"Put this crystal in your pocket. It can close a portal. And put this one around your neck to capture what some call a shadow being. Now look in the drawer over there," she said pointing.

C.W looked in and saw what looked to be a wrapped up piece of cake. "What you think I can eat now?" he asked.

"That's an energy bar, fool, for the soul to see past this physical world. Kush has nothing on this, Bro," she said smiling.

C.W pocketed it, then went to his room closet for a 45 automatic and two extra clips.

"I have one grenade, Divine. If I tell you to leave, just run 'cause it may be the only way to stop them, and I need to know you will do as I say," he said sternly.

"I will." She grabbed two ninja-like swords and a belt of small blades. "Damn, Divine, you can use them?" He was both proud and amazed. Before he could laugh, she cut the cake in half and replaced the sword in its holster on her side.

"Oh shit! My damn sister a ninja!" She followed him out to the truck. He cranked the car up and ate half the cake while Divine got the music together: Nas and Damian Marley.

"Skeeta, we coming to get you, brother."

"This some real powerful shit," C.W. said.

"It's called the Bread of a Warrior. Men are given this before their rites of passage. It contains everything from peyote to kush to mushroom and some other powerful herbs. You should be feeling the Warrior very soon. Oh, and remember our Tai Chi classes? Focus there."

"The sun going down," he said, turning to the backstreet towards the house.

"Breathe deeply and remember that they feed on fears, so remain strong. And listen out for Mama. She's here too."

He drove right into the doorway. "Divine, they waiting on us." She nodded.

He proceeded to give her instructions. "Check?" He needed her to be focused and obedient.

"Check, I'll be right behind you," she answered.

"The girl Vanity came to me in a vision. She's lost, but I keep seeing you with her. Remember that she's lost too, okay?"

He nodded then backed out the driveway into the wooded area in front of the house. Divine rolled out unseen. C.W. gassed up to about 50 mph and through the front door. As the truck came to a stop, all you could hear was the engine running and the sound of Nas and Damian Marley echoing through the house. Feeling a little shaken up, he recalled his sister's advice to breathe deeply and fear not.

"Vanity, you can take me and let go of my friend," he said, moving to the wall with the AK held in military position. A shadow moved in the corner. He shot, but nothing fell. As he moved deeper in the house, the same candles were present. Without thinking, he got down on the floor and began covering himself in blood. The shadows grew closer. He removed the crystal from his pocket and raised it in the air.

The first one that moved upon him was captured in the crystal. The power of the shadow being transferred to C.W. He could feel the strength moving and settling in his body. Moving down the hall, he realized that he now had the power to move and blend like the shadow beings.

"Cee, mother named you Wisdom. It is the key to your gift. It is the application of knowledge, and so it is. Motion. Allow your power to cause motion of all things," Divine telepathically spoke to C.W.

Because of the blood on C.W, the shadows couldn't help but draw to him. Every time they did so, the crystal captured them. As the power charged in C.W, a sixth sense made him throw his dagger straight up without looking in a motion so fast he shocked himself. A werewolf fell from the ceiling with the dagger in its head. He reclaimed his tool and continued down the long hall.

"Vanity, I sense you're afraid!" He yelled out, trying to provoke her.

Instead of her emerging, three of the robed elders came forth. The one in the middle held a candle. They pulled back their hoods and began growling. Their white eyes lit up the dark hallway. As C.W raised his gun to shoot, the one in the middle threw the candle at him. It transformed into a ball of fire. He ducked, and when he went to stand up, the other two rushed him, knocking him down and the gun out of his hand.

In one swift, Tai Chi motion, C.W. slid across the floor on his stomach, pushed himself up to this feet, and threw a ball of energy back at them. Two of the men flew back, but quickly recollected and took off down the hall.

"Don't run now!" C.W. yelled. He was ready for war. Hearing and feeling heavy breathing behind him, he turned around to face two more werewolves running towards him. Divine dropped down from the ceiling, slicing their heads off in like a one clean motion.

"Go," she ordered as she disappeared back in the dark.

"Go? What the fuck you mean go?"She didn't answer and when he turned around, Vanity kicked him in the chest. He landed in another room and as he tried to get up, she blew a handful of powder in his face. He lost consciousness and the elders picked him up.

"Cee, wake up, wake up!" cried Skeeta.

"Please," he begged.

C.W. begins to come back around only to find that he and Skeeta are tied down to some type of ceremonial table.

"You came back, man. I kept saying Cee ain't gonna leave me. He ain't gon' leave me. I love you, Cee." Skeeta made no effort to hide or stop his tears.

C.W. was too busy plotting to be emotional. He looked around and spotted his dagger on another table by the wall. He tried to use his mind to bring the dagger to him, but it didn't move.

"Damn, this shit don't work," he said to himself.

"What shit? I know you called the police, right?" Skeeta asked. Realizing that C.W. didn't answer him, he asked again, "You called the police?" He felt himself growing more frantic.

"It works. You're just in a binding circle. Everything inside is bound. Two different worlds. So now your poor little sister is all alone. Call her so she can watch you die. Poor, Divine," Vanity said, laughing.

"No!" C.W. yelled. He tried to break free, but couldn't.

"Cee, you didn't call the police?" Skeeta asked desperately.

"NO, SKEETA!""Cee, they cutting heads off and you didn't call the police?"

"No, Skeeta. He didn't," Vanity spoke.

"He and Divine came to save you. So sweet, yet so dumb."

"What happened to you? So beautiful, but yet so ugly inside. But it's not ugly, it's pain, and something is eating on that pain. You weren't born for this, not with the face of a goddess," C.W. reasoned.

"I was born just for this. My mother was one of them. Like me, she was evil and practiced Black Magic. She died giving birth to me. I came here killing. I killed my own mom! It's not pain. It's my nature to kill. I was born with a thirst for blood. A Jesuit monk told me of my mother's evil ways and Jesuit's gave me to my powerful family to help me find my place. A family who were more willing to help me understand my evil, I mean my different nature, that not even the Priest could," said Vanity smiling.

"Miss Emerald died giving birth to Divine, but she's not evil and she different too," Skeeta added.

"Right, Skeeta. Vanity, you're not evil. You one of us. Listen, they are tricking you. All sacred mothers died giving birth to the chosen daughters, The Seven Sacred Vessels. Your mother wasn't evil. She was a high priestess; the Jesuit was one of evil ones trying to trick you. Ever wondered why they needed you? It's because you are the only one who can sense us out. They need you to destroy your family—"

"—Wrong! There are only six vessels and I've already killed two. Plus—" She was interrupted by a voice that could only be compared to a storm.

"SILENCE!"Vanity trembled in fear."Look, Vanity. They trying to stop you from realizing. You have an older brother, don't you? He is older than you and when you came, she died. My mother did the same, but she left a guide for us. I know you feel me because your heart asked me to help you find your way. The day you held my hand to your heart," C.W. said before being silenced by the voice. The same voice vibrating in power pinned him to the table, choking him.

"It's not true," Vanity said, running off. Once released, C.W looked over at Skeeta and realized that he still had the golden dagger that he'd grabbed from the wall.

CHAPTER SEVEN: THE DAGGER OF DESTINY

C.W attempted to warn Divine, through his thoughts, that they wanted her and was using him as bait. He turned his focus over to the dagger on Skeeta's belt.

"Oh shit, Cee! Something crawling on me!" Skeeta cried, feeling the dagger moving.

"Be quiet," he ordered. C.W. grabbed the blade from the air and used it to stab the candle. The binding cords loosened and released Skeeta and C.W. from its grip.

"C.W, you did that or is this a trick?"Ignoring him to focus on the task at hand, C.W. picked up the knife.

"C.W., we got a problem," said Skeeta. Two monks stood before them.

"Shoot!" C.W said and dived out the way. Skeeta fired off, but the monks were moving too fast, dodging each bullet. C.W. charges at one, but is knocked across the room where he passes out. Skeeta runs to help, but is cut off by a monk. From beneath the robe, he raised his hand, which looked like the claw of an animal. Just as he swung at Skeeta, his head dropped and his arm fell to the ground.

"Skeeta you can open your eyes now," a woman's voice said.

"I don't want to."

"We have to hurry, Skeeta. There's not much time," the woman said.

"Oh God, I'm about to die," Skeeta cried. He peeked through one eye and saw Vanity.

"No you're not. Now let's get C.W up," she said, lifting C.W.'s head from the floor. Skeeta looked around and saw the two monks were both beheaded.

"This dream is too long. Why can't I just wake up?" he said. He went over to help.

"Come on, C.W.," Vanity pleaded, looking around in fear.

"Just do the movie shit and kiss him. He'll wake up. This my dream," suggested Skeeta. Vanity kissed him so passionately that Skeeta had to lean over for a closer look.

"You meant that one, didn't you?" he asked. C.W. opened his eyes.

"Shit, it worked!" said Skeeta.

"What happened?" C.W. asked, shaking his head.

"Just a head injury," Vanity answered.Realizing who he was talking to, he jumped up/"No, Cee, she saved us this time. She still scares me too though," said Skeeta. "Cee, you were right about everything. I was so lost. I never met anyone like me. I thought I was evil. Please allow me to help. I know everything you need to know," she pleaded. For once, her eyes were sincere.

"How can I be sure it's not a trick?" C.W. asked.

"Ask your heart. It seems to know mine," she answered, then dropped her head.

"She dropped her head. I remember that one. Hell no," Skeeta said, shaking his head.

"No, Skeeta. A woman does it out of shame, when they speak truth," C.W. said walking closer to her.

"This ain't the time," Skeeta warned C.W. He stepped between them and looked C.W. square in the eye with one brow raised.

"He's right. Let's go," said Vanity.

"I gotta find my sister," C.W. said.

"They are going to create an astral opening to pull your mother and use her to capture your sister. Your sister is too powerful, so they have to trick her off this plane. They need your blood to do this. It's a type of birthing process, if you will," Vanity explained. Out of nowhere, a dagger knocks her down.

"Shit!" Skeeta yelled, running to the other side of the room. C.W. moved like a shadow being, dodging their blades. He threw a ball of light, knocking the attacking monks into another dimension.

"Damn, you move like them!" Skeeta said.

"Is she alive?" C.W. asked.

"Yeah, look like she only got hit in the arm," Skeeta said.

"Lay her down for now. We gotta find Divine before they do," said C.W.Howling sounds echoed throughout the house. The rumble of a storm followed. The candles began violently flickering again.

"Oh, shit! They coming!" Skeeta yelled, hiding behind C.W.

The whole wall blew off in an explosion, revealing the dimensional gate. Gruesome forms surrounded the gateway. Behind it stood a tree and three monks with stones like coffins marked with ancient symbols.

"Cee, I don't think Divine here. Let's go," Skeeta whimpered, holding onto the back of C.W.'s shirt.

"Skeeta, I don't think they going to let us go like that."

"Thy life is required as the holy offering. A boundless number of beings will enter this realm to claim it. You will cause destruction of all. Unless you come now. Your life for your sister's life." As the voice spoke, more and more beings lined up at the gateway. The monks opened the stone coffin and raised Divine.

"No!" yelled C.W. He ran forward, but couldn't cross over.

"Remove the daggers and lie on the table of ceremony."

"Cee, it may be a trick. Don't go. Please," begged Skeeta.

"Skeeta, they already won." C.W. dropped the daggers. The table of ceremony rose from the ground in front of the monks and the tree. C.W walked forward then stopped.

"Before I do, let my sister go."

"She will be freed as you finish our blood ceremony and she will provide for us too."

C.W. was forced onto the table. The monks came forth and stabbed him in his hands and feet. His blood drained into the sacred matter. He laid there paralyzed, feeling his life force leaving his body. In a glowing light, he saw Vanity in a bridal dress being lifted and carried to another table.

"The blood of the son, the priestess, and the daughter is the complete flame of life to bring thy majesty forward. The daughter must be brought forth now," the monks chanted. Another table rose next to C.W, and Divine was placed on it.

"My son, you must find your power here. Your sister needs you. I need you." C.W.'s mother's voice was so close it was as if she was there.

"Divine, please hear me," C.W. thought.

"When they go to stick your hand, move. You may be able to grab the dagger from them." But she didn't move. *If Divine is next to me then who is that in the stone coffin?*

"Let the Ancient One be raised," the dominant voice stated. The monks responded by raising the daggers towards Divine's hands.

"One more prayer," Skeeta said, picking up the dagger. Several werewolves surround him.

The priest cut Divine's left hand and blood drained down the ceremony table. The cry of the beast sounded like a thousand explosions. The world trembled and the monks began to remove their hoods and bow their heads. A seven-foot monk in a white robe rose from the ground and spoke: "The blood of the son and of the daughter will prepare the one to take the bride. And the Wheel of Destiny will be returned to our rule forever!" A bolt of lightning punctuated his sentence.

"*They need you and your sister's blood to break the Wheel of Destiny. The chosen bride must not marry the beast he seeks a host into the physical. They possess the parallel, and we will be lost forever,*" said C.W.'s mother. He doesn't move.

"Please, God, one more," Skeeta said. He threw the dagger at the monk just before he could cut Divine's other hand. The knife flew slowly through the air stabbing the monk in the back causing him to throw his knife in the air. The flipped up in the air from the monk's hand into the air like an angel with wings, then came back down and pierced him in the eye. The binding spell breaks and both C.W. and Divine jumps up.

The lead monk ran to attack. Divine grabbed the dagger and in one swift motion, threw it at him. He blocked it with his staff. She continued her attack, but he disappeared only to reappear right before her and grab her by the throat. C.W. ran to help and was snatched and lifted by his throat as well. Then the ground began to tremble. A concrete cross the size of a small building rose from beneath the ceremony table. The grand monk walked towards it holding C.W. and Divine.

"Great Majesty, I will deliver to you the blood of the host from my hand," said the Grand Monk as he slowly began to claw into the necks of his victims. Blood dripped onto the stone cross. It opened and a beast as never before seen began to rise, having a woman's head, man's body, and wolf's legs and tail. It was one of the Ancients that was trapped in the Astral after the meteorite shower that bound himself in the lower nature but still contained......its Ancient power.

"Our rulers from the astral will, by the blood of the son and daughter, gain entrance and close the astral Wheel of Marriage of the Priestess Auset", says the Grand Monk as he squeezed his claws deeper into their flesh. The beast gained power and changed form. As he began to rise, lightning struck and thunder boomed. The gateway glowed like Mars, of a reddish hue, and started to cross over to the other side.

"Conscious, remember the control here can shape frequency of the Earth. Rise, Conscious, arise," said Emerald as the stone coffin closed her.

"One of many, and soon to be ruler of ALL," said the Grand Monk as blood of C.W and Divine drained down his arm to the mouth of the beast. Then the Grand Monk fell flat on his face and the beast devoured him. Divine and C.W. looked at one another confused, then saw Vanity standing there holding a dagger. The beast jumped out of the cross and lunged towards them. C.W. tried to use his force, but it did nothing to slow it down. Divine and C.W were cornered by the tree. Then Vanity threw another dagger, piercing it in the head. Instead of killing it, the beast became enraged and turned to attack her.

"Escape now, Divine!" yelled C.W. Without thinking, he ran to Vanity's side at the speed of light. He took the medicine bag and sprinkled its contents around them. Though the beast tried, he couldn't enter.

"We don't have long before he can break through it. By that time, Divine will be out." He held Vanity in his arms.

"I understand, but why did you save me?"

"Love makes us do dumb things sometimes." He blushed, then pulled out the crystal.

"What's that?"

"The only way to close the portal. But it will close most likely with us too." His nose brushed against hers.

"My mother named me Auset," she said softly, eyes closed.

"Are you ready, Auset?" He held the crystal as he watched the circle weaken.

"I am, my love," she answered. As C.W threw the crystal down, a burst of blue-white light came forth and the beast was pulled back into the cross. Everything went dark. Cries were the only sounds being made. They felt like they were floating in a vacuum of space where time didn't exist.

Auset heard her mother speak: *"My dear, Auset, I knew you would make it. Now follow your destiny. You will be the first of the new age."* Then in the midst of darkness, as C.W and Auset held hands, her mother appeared in a golden form and kissed the top of her head. Auset fell to her knees, crying tears of pure happiness. C.W.'s parents appeared next. *"Our children, forever keep and protect the way."* Then like a comet, they all disappeared.

Auset and C.W held each other. "How do we return, Conscious," asked Auset.

"It's funny, but I know the answer. It's by Love," said Conscious as he kissed Auset. Their hearts of truth united like the helix of DNA and like a ladder they climbed higher and higher in pure spiritual climax until their souls touched. The Universe stood still and the sacred OM hummed its infinite sound. They fell from the opening, through the ceiling, and onto the floor, right in front of Skeeta and Divine.

"You two scared the shit out of me," said Skeeta as he ran to hug C.W.

"Cee, you did it! You are my hero!" said Divine as she ran to him too. C.W and Auset both stood and hugged, and then C.W hugged Divine and Skeeta.

A bookshelf fell by them and everyone jumped. "Let's get out of here before something else happens," suggested C.W. and everyone shook their head in agreement.

C.W. walked out, holding Auset's hand. The truck still sat in the foyer. Skeeta and C.W. pushed it out of the house and Divine got inside to crank it up. They all jumped in to leave and C.W. grabbed a grenade and tossed it inside the house.

"Just to make sure," he said.

As Auset held C.W.'s hand, Skeeta look and asked "What you too had time to find something".

They both laughed, and Divine looked and smiled. "This so crazy, 'cause I am still scared of Vanity. So you two gonna have to help me. I saw too much today."

"Skeeta, it's alright. She didn't know, and her name is Auset," C.W. said, tapping Skeeta on the shoulder.

"Now the girl don' changed her name to Aw-shit. I know this too much."

"No, Skeeta. *Auset*," Divine and C.W. said at the same time, laughing. "Please don't yell at me. I don't know. But even though all this fucked up shit don' happened, and I found out that C.W is really X-Men and now he married to the devil's wife, I still feel today was special 'cause I prayed for the first time and everything came true. I prayed for a sister and I got one. Then I prayed for C.W. to come back and get me, and damn...Y'all still working that stuff? I couldn't even talk. I prayed C.W. would come back and get me 'cause them people ain't want me. And I'll be damned if Cee ain't come back. My life forever changed. I saw a real bitch, so I won't call my beautiful sisters bitches no more. Shit, I think I'm going to stop eating meat for the rest of my life. Divine, you gonna have to teach me how to make barbecue celery sticks."

Everyone laughed. They stopped at a traffic light and that's when the reality of all they'd survived hit them. *Boom! Boom!* A hand hit the window and everyone jumped."Hey, you know all your back lights out. You better get off the road before you get pulled over," said a random guy.

"Thank you, man. But don't ever run your ass up on a car like that 'cause a nigga will blow your bitch ass head off, feel me?" Skeeta said, lowering the window with the gun in his hand. The guy ran back to his car. Everyone looked at Skeeta and shook their head.

"Well, I said I was going to work on it. So give me a minute 'cause he scared the pee out of me. Made me think about the movies when the people think they got away then something happens. So I am going to be truthful before I get bad luck. C.W, Divine and Aw- shit—I mean, Auset— while that damn portal was closing, I ran to the safe to hide and while I was in there, I grabbed cash and about five gold bars and this silver too," he said opening his bag.

"Skeeta, that's not silver. That's platinum! You have about five million there," said Auset. Everyone laughed and Skeeta began to cry.

"Why you crying, Skeeta?" asked Divine.

"'Cause I know I got to share this with y'all and now ain't no more Vanity," he whined.

"Why is that a bad thing?" asked Divine.

"'Cause I really wanted to...let's just say I had a dream that one day little boys could find little exotic girls and be friends."

"I guess this is where we part," said Auset after they pulled into the front yard.

"No, I don't. That's our destiny. Plus, I don' think love works like that," said C.W.

"So that means you still want me to stay," she asked hesitantly.

"Yeah, girl. Plus, it's not over. We have to find the other three Sacred Ones," said Divine.

"After all that I've done. Are you sure, Cee?"

"All you did was make us all realize our divine destiny," he said, pulling her closer.

"C.W., let the girl come on in so I can fix her arm up. You know you was stabbed, don't you? Love is good, but in another hour, you will be in pain," Divine reminded him.

"OWW!" yelled Skeeta. Everyone ran over, thinking something wrong.

"What's wrong, Skee?" C.W. asked with his gun drawn.

"This cake you had in your truck is the damn real deal. I see spirits," Skeeta said with a big smile across his face.Everyone laughed and headed in the house.

"Divine, thank you," said Auset as they walked in."

"No, thank you. For now, our lives have begun."

Skeeta before walking in the house looks up at the sky and pours his drink on the ground as he says, "Splack, family, you not forgotten. I felt your death but I also felt your life." They all walked straight to the meditation room, took a seat, and just looked at one another. Together, they accepted that the journey had just started and was far from over.

And this is how the travels of the two sacred queens began. The hidden keepers of the way, the children of the sacred vessels, are always amongst us, guarding the Wheel of Destiny. Their stories are our stories of life and the truth behind the many illusions we live on the flat line. Once the dimensions are revealed to us, life will never be the same.

TO BE CONTINUED...

Made in the USA
Monee, IL
03 March 2020